UNiCORN ACADEMY

Blaze and Scarlett finally reached the top of the glacier. Below them, Unicorn Island stretched out far into the distance. Scarlett was filled with a mixture of wonder and pride. This was her home. She had to save it!

LOOK OUT FOR MORE ADVENTURES AT

UNICORN ACADEMY

Sophia and Rainbow
Scarlett and Blaze
Ava and Star
Isabel and Cloud
Layla and Dancer
Olivia and Snowflake

JULIE SYKES

illustrated by LUCY TRUMAN

A STEPPING STONE BOOK™

Random House New York

For April

 Published in the United States by Random House Children's Books, a division of Penguin Random House LLC, New York.
Originally published in paperback by Nosy Crow Ltd, London, in 2018.

Random House and the colophon are registered trademarks and A Stepping Stone Book and the colophon are trademarks of Penguin Random House LLC.

Visit us on the Web! rhcbooks.com

Educators and librarians, for a variety of teaching tools,
visit us at RHTeachersLibrarians.com

Library of Congress Cataloging-in-Publication Data
Names: Sykes, Julie, author. | Truman, Lucy, illustrator.
Title: Scarlett and Blaze / Julie Sykes; illustrated by Lucy Truman.
Description: First American edition. | New York: Random House, 2019. |
Series: Unicorn Academy; #2 | Originally published in London by Nosy Crow in 2018. | Summary: "Magical Sparkle Lake is starting to freeze, and Unicorn Academy might have to close. Can ten-year-old Scarlett and her unicorn Blaze find out who's freezing the lake and save the school?"
Identifiers: LCCN 2018027747 | ISBN 978-1-9848-5085-0 (paperback) |
ISBN 978-1-9848-5086-7 (hardcover library binding) |
ISBN 978-1-9848-5087-4 (ebook)
Subjects: | CYAC: Unicorns—Fiction. | Magic—Fiction. | Boarding schools—Fiction. | Schools—Fiction.
Classification: LCC PZ7.S98325 Sc 2019 | DDC [Fic]—dc23

Printed in the United States of America
10 9 8 7 6 5 4 3 2 1
First American Edition

Random House Children's Books supports the First Amendment
and celebrates the right to read.

CHAPTER 1

"Higher!" said Scarlett.

Isabel, Scarlett's best friend, raised the branch again, balancing it carefully between a bush and the gnarled trunk of an old tree. It was as high as her head now.

"I think that's too big," said Cloud, Isabel's unicorn, giving the jump a doubtful look.

Scarlett pushed her long blond hair back over her shoulders. Her blue eyes sparkled as she patted her own unicorn's neck. Her cheeks were flushed from the icy breeze, and snowflakes whirled around her.

"It's not too big for us, is it, Blaze?"

"Definitely not. I can clear that easily!" Blaze whickered. The cheeky-looking unicorn with fiery red-and-gold swirls on her snow-white coat loved a challenge, just like Scarlett. "Watch this, Cloud!"

Blaze galloped eagerly at the makeshift jump. Scarlett sank her hands deeper into Blaze's silky mane as she took off, the crisp air making her eyes water. Scarlett loved the feeling of flying and then plunging back down to earth. As Blaze landed, a

few orange sparks flickered up from her hooves and Scarlett caught a faint whiff of burnt sugar.

Isabel gasped. "That was incredible. You jumped so high, I almost thought you were going to fly away!"

Scarlett's heart skipped with hope—the huge jump, the sparks, and the sweet smell. Could that mean Blaze was about to discover her magic power? Every unicorn on Unicorn Island was born with a special magical power—it just took a while for that power to be revealed. Some unicorns could fly, others turned invisible, some could create light or fire. Scarlett couldn't wait for Blaze to discover her power, and she really hoped it would be flying.

Scarlett was ten years old and had recently started at Unicorn Academy, where she had been given her own special unicorn, just like all the other girls and boys who had joined at the same time. They were all in training to become full-fledged guardians of Unicorn Island, the wonderful land in which they lived.

Scarlett knew she would be able to move up at the end of the year only if Blaze had discovered her magical power and bonded with her. She let her hair fall forward, searching for a red-gold lock of hair to match Blaze's mane that would show they had bonded. But there was no flame-colored strand in her long blond hair yet. Disappointed, Scarlett turned her attention back to the jump.

"Put it up even higher," she called, hoping that if it was big enough, Blaze might actually fly!

"I'll put it up in a minute. It's my turn first," said Isabel, turning Cloud to face the jump. Cloud was a pretty unicorn with gentle brown eyes.

"I think it's too big for me, Isabel," said Cloud anxiously.

"No, it's not," said Isabel. "Blaze jumped it easily. Let's try!"

"Wait, Isabel!" whispered Scarlett as she spotted Ms. Nettles, one of the teachers, cantering over on her unicorn, Thyme.

Isabel ignored her. "Don't be boring, Cloud! Come on. Give it a try!"

"Isabel!" insisted Scarlett. "Behind you!" Of all the teachers to catch them jumping, Ms. Nettles was the worst. She was very strict, with a fierce temper.

"Isabel!" Ms. Nettles's sharp voice rang out, giving Isabel a shock. "I hope that you were not about to jump that!" Ms. Nettles's glasses rattled on her bony nose as her unicorn halted.

"Of . . . of course not, Ms. Nettles," Isabel said quickly. "We were just making jumps, not jumping them."

"Definitely not jumping them," said Scarlett, shaking her head.

Ms. Nettles gave them a suspicious look. "You'd better be telling the truth, girls. You know the rules. First years are not allowed to jump without a teacher to supervise."

Thyme, her unicorn, nodded, his green-and-yellow tail swishing along with his head.

Scarlett swallowed back a giggle.

"It's for your own safety, so please abide by the rule. Now, it's almost dinnertime," Ms. Nettles continued. "Ride back to the stables with me."

"Yes, Ms. Nettles," the girls sighed.

Scarlett felt bad that Isabel hadn't gotten her turn at the jump. "Sorry," she mouthed.

"Next time," Isabel whispered back. They gave each other a thumbs-up behind the teacher's back. Scarlett felt a rush of happiness. She and Isabel had been friends since day one. They both loved riding fast and jumping high, although Isabel was much more competitive than Scarlett—she loved to win, whereas Scarlett didn't care who won just as long as she was having fun.

The February sun was almost on the horizon as they neared the school building. The wintry rays lit up the magnificent pink-marble and colored-glass building, making it glow as if it were on fire.

"Unicorn Academy," Scarlett sighed happily. "It's so beautiful, especially now that it's snowing."

Her eyes moved from the grandness of the tall towers to the graceful curve of the domed roofs, then across the huge lawn to the multicolored lake with a tall fountain glittering at the center. The magical waters of Sparkle Lake flowed up from the center of the earth through the fountain, before rivers took it all over Unicorn Island. Every unicorn on the island drank its water every day to strengthen their magic and stay healthy.

"Unicorn Academy is the best school ever," agreed Isabel proudly. She shivered. "Brrrr, it's *soooo* cold. Look at the snowflakes landing on the lake. It must be freezing over."

"Imagine the fun we'll have if the lake does freeze," said Scarlett. "We can go ice skating."

Ms. Nettles's head whipped around. "Don't talk nonsense, girls! Sparkle Lake has never frozen over in the history of Unicorn Academy. It will take more than a cold snap to freeze its waters."

Isabel scrunched up her eyes against the low winter sun. "But it's so cold. Isn't there a tiny chance it could freeze?"

"It is unusually cold, I agree," said Ms. Nettles. "But I am sure the lake will withstand the temperature drop. If Sparkle Lake did freeze, it would mean the unicorns would be unable to drink the water they need, and that would be a disaster for the island. You would certainly not be allowed to ice skate! You're here to learn how to protect it—not to play on it! Now, stop chattering and take your unicorns into the stables and feed them. Be quick. If you're late for dinner, you shall clean my riding boots as punishment. Go on!"

As Ms. Nettles rode away toward the lake, Scarlett saw her pull a little bottle from her pocket, and the corners of the teacher's mouth turned up into a smile.

"What's she up to?" Scarlett wondered aloud. "She never smiles!"

"Who cares?" said Isabel. "How about a race?"

Scarlett immediately forgot about Ms. Nettles and grinned. "Why not! Last one back is a rotten egg!"

"It won't be us!" shouted Isabel. She and Cloud galloped full speed toward the stables.

"Go, Blaze!" Scarlett cried.

Blaze's breath spurted out clouds in the icy air as they gave chase, but they couldn't quite catch Cloud with her head start.

"We won!" said Isabel, punching the air in triumph. "Go, us!"

Scarlett didn't care. It had been a fun race even if Isabel had beaten her. "That was amazing," she said, sliding off and hugging Blaze. "Thank you, Blaze! You're the best unicorn here!"

Blaze nuzzled Scarlett back, her dark eyes shining happily.

CHAPTER 2

The lights in the stable glowed softly. The heated floor was so lovely and warm that Scarlett unwound her scarf and stuffed her red gloves in her pocket. She hopped clear of a remote-controlled cart as it went trundling past with a big container of sky berries—the special berries from the mountains behind the school that the unicorns loved to eat.

Blaze went into her stall and drank from her silver water trough. Each unicorn had their own trough that magically filled with water from the lake.

"Delicious!" Blaze smacked her lips, but as she went to take another drink, she snorted in alarm. "Where did the water go? My trough's not refilling!"

"What's that?" Scarlett broke off chattering with Isabel.

"My trough's broken." Blaze rattled it with her muzzle.

"It can't be." The individual water troughs in the stalls and the main troughs in the stable aisles never ran out of lake water. Scarlett went into Blaze's stall and put her hand under the water spout. Water suddenly spurted everywhere. She squealed. "Blaze! You tricked me!"

"No, I didn't!" Blaze protested.

Scarlett giggled and flicked water over her. "I actually believed you for a moment."

"I wasn't joking, Scarlett." Blaze stared at the water trough. "It wasn't working."

Scarlett just laughed. "Stop messing around. You'll make me late."

"I'm not messing around," Blaze said. "I saw some ice crystals in the water."

"Ice crystals? Where?" Scarlett kept her distance, expecting Blaze to shower her with water if she went too close.

"They've melted now," said Blaze.

"Of course they have." Scarlett chuckled. "Right, I'm going to get you some berries."

She returned a few minutes later with a bucket full of sky berries and plonked it on the floor. Blaze gobbled them up hungrily. Scarlett stroked her, twisting her fingers in a swirl of red-and-gold mane that reminded her of a flame. "I'll see you in the morning," she said. "It's the weekend, so no lessons, just fun! I'm going to braid your mane and tail with gold ribbons my big sisters sent me."

"Your family spoils you rotten!" laughed Isabel, peeking around Blaze's stall door.

"A box of chocolates came from the boys this morning too." Scarlett smiled. She was the youngest of five. Her older brothers and sisters were always sending her treats. "I'll share them with our dorm."

"Awesome. But we'd better get a move on now," said Isabel, glancing at the clock on the wall. "I don't want to clean Ms. Nettles's stinky boots."

"Me neither," agreed Scarlett. She gave Blaze a final hug, and then she and Isabel hurried back to the school, arm in arm.

★

The next day was even colder. When the girls woke, there was a thin layer of snow and ice on Sapphire dorm's window. Scarlett stayed in bed, curled up in her blue-and-silver blanket like a mouse until Isabel whipped it away.

"You're mean!" Scarlett's teeth chattered.

"Catch me if you can!" shouted Isabel. She looked like a glittery ghost as she circled the room with the blanket draped over her shoulders.

Scarlett chased after her with a pillow, bopping Isabel on the head with it. Isabel ditched the blanket and grabbed a pillow to bop her back.

"Pillow fight!" yelled Sophia, getting out of bed.

Olivia and Ava jumped up to join in. Quieter Layla got dressed with a worried frown on her

face as the other five girls in Sapphire dorm ran around, bashing each other with feathery pillows.

"Phew! I'm too hot now," gasped Scarlett, lying on her bed.

"Me too!" said Isabel, collapsing beside her.

"You can't just lie there," said Layla. "There are feathers everywhere. You'd better clean them up before breakfast, or we'll all be in trouble."

"What are you doing today, Sophia?" Scarlett said, ignoring Layla, who she thought was rather boring. Layla sighed and started cleaning up the feathers herself.

"Ava and I are going to look for some spring bulbs and herbs to plant in her garden," said Sophia, holding her black hair off her neck to cool down. "Then we'll go for a long ride around the grounds. I promised Rainbow he could have a good gallop today. How about you two?"

"Riding, jumping, and avoiding Ms. Nettles," said Scarlett.

"I want to sneak onto the cross-country course," said Isabel.

"Just don't get caught like Billy and Lightning did," warned Ava. "They weren't allowed to go riding together for three days as punishment!"

Scarlett bubbled with happiness as she pulled on her riding clothes and red hoodie. Lessons were okay, but she much preferred the weekend, when she didn't have to learn anything. She was really looking forward to hanging out with Isabel and their unicorns, braiding Blaze's mane and tail with the sparkly gold ribbons, and going riding, of course.

"There are enough ribbons for you and Cloud to have some," she told Isabel as they walked to the stables together after a delicious breakfast of bacon, eggs, sweet pastries, and fresh fruit. "But

let's braid their manes and tails first—I'm much too full to ride right now. I feel like I'm going to pop!"

"The food here is so yummy," said Isabel. "My mom said that when it's warmer, you're allowed packed lunches on the weekend. We can go for long rides and have picnics, explore the mountains, and maybe use magic!"

Scarlett smiled. Her older brothers and sisters had always come back from Unicorn Academy with incredible stories of the adventures and fun they'd had getting to know their unicorns and discovering their magical power. Now that she was a student with her very own unicorn, she was finding out that school was just as amazing as they'd said. She couldn't wait to discover Blaze's power and bond with her. Then their adventures would be even better!

As they entered the stables, Scarlett was

surprised to see the unicorns crowding around the main drinking trough. They were whickering unhappily and stamping their hooves. Some students were anxiously peering into the drinking troughs and water spouts.

"What's going on?" she said.

Isabel frowned. "I don't know, but it looks serious. We'd better find out."

CHAPTER 3

Scarlett and Isabel squeezed between the unicorns to reach Blaze and Cloud.

"Scarlett!" Blaze whinnied in relief. "Thank goodness you're here. The drinking troughs have frozen. I'm so thirsty, and my head aches. Can you get me some water from the lake?"

"Of course," said Scarlett, but before she could go anywhere, the elderly head teacher, Ms. Primrose, came into the stable with her golden unicorn, Sage. Ms. Primrose was wrapped up warmly in a thick hoodie, two scarves, and a pair of pink-and-gold riding boots.

"Good morning, everyone," she said. "As you can see, the weather has turned extremely cold, and for the first time in living memory, the lake has started to freeze."

Isabel gasped, and Scarlett's face reddened as she remembered how yesterday she'd thought that it might be fun if the lake did freeze for a bit. Ms. Primrose clapped her hands, silencing the chatter.

"If the lake continues to freeze, then there won't be any water for the unicorns to drink. That would be dreadful. All the unicorns would become ill and lose their magic powers."

Scarlett glanced at Blaze. She'd already complained of a headache. She might get very sick if she couldn't drink the lake water. Scarlett began to listen more carefully.

"We must collect as much water as possible," Ms. Primrose went on. "I've arranged for some specially heated storage containers to be put in the stables. No matter what the temperature is outside, the stored water won't freeze. Unfortunately, these containers need to be filled by hand. Go and collect the others from your dorm, and make sure each of you takes a bucket from your advisor. Then start transferring water from the lake to the containers. The harder you work, the sooner the job will be done. Off you go, now."

As Ms. Primrose left the stables with Sage, everyone started talking at once.

"What will happen to Unicorn Island if the lake freezes?"

"How will the island survive?"

Scarlett patted Blaze's neck. Now that she knew there was enough water to last for a few days, she felt more relaxed about the lake freezing for a little while. "Let's not worry about it, Blaze. Ms. Nettles said the lake will never freeze completely, and even if it does, we'll have collected enough water to last until it thaws again. Let's enjoy the snow and frost! It'll be great fun playing in it!"

★

It was hard work, fetching water from the lake and carrying it to the containers in the stables. The thin layer of snow covering the ground grew slushy, splashing Scarlett's legs as she walked back and forth. Her initial enthusiasm quickly wore off, until she was spending more time chatting with Isabel than working. It took the whole morning before the containers were full.

"I'm not doing that again," panted Scarlett,

dumping her bucket outside Blaze's stall rather than walk the extra steps to put it back in the storeroom.

"I doubt we'll have to," said Isabel. "It feels warmer now—the sun's coming out."

Warmed by the pale winter sun, the afternoon was much more fun. Scarlett brushed Blaze's mane, not exactly until it shone, but enough to get the tangles out. Then she braided the gold ribbons through it. Blaze's tail proved a little harder, with a wisp of hair that refused to lie flat. Spying the bucket she'd left outside the stable, Scarlett grabbed it to get some water from the drinking trough to tame the flyaway hair. To her surprise, the water in the trough was covered in ice, and Scarlett had to chip it away to reach the water beneath it.

"Watch out, clumsy!" Valentina de Silva shouted at Scarlett as she swept by with her two annoying friends. "You just splashed me." Valentina gave Scarlett a haughty look. Not only was she Ms. Nettles's niece, but she thought she was better than anyone else at Unicorn Academy because her parents were school directors.

"Oh dear," said Scarlett, deliberately swinging the bucket into the air so the icy water splashed Valentina. "Whoops, sorry, Valentina. I really am clumsy today!" She chuckled as water dripped from Valentina's brown hair.

"That's it! I'm telling!" shrieked Valentina, storming off to find a teacher. Her two friends gave Scarlett an angry look before scurrying after Valentina.

"Scarlett, please stop wasting water!" begged Layla, coming out of Dancer's stall. "What will our unicorns drink if the lake freezes for more than a few days? Do you want them to get sick?"

Seeing Layla's serious expression, Scarlett

blushed. It was hard for her to be serious about anything, and annoying snooty Valentina was great fun, but she hadn't meant to put the unicorns at risk, especially dear Blaze. "You worry too much!" she said to Layla, but after that she only took a small amount of water from the drinking trough, and she walked slowly so as not to spill any as she carried it back to Blaze.

★

That evening in the students' lounge everyone wanted to talk about the lake and what would happen if it froze over.

"We might get sent home," said Olivia, her green eyes round with concern.

"The lake won't freeze," scoffed Isabel, warming her hands on the blazing log fire. "You're all worrying about nothing. It's not cold enough."

"It's not cold in here," said Ava, her chin-length dark hair framing her face. "But it's freezing

outside. The teachers are really worried. I heard Ms. Nettles talking to herself earlier. She was muttering something about spells and the lake, but she went silent when she saw me."

"That's odd," said Sophia.

"Not really. Ms. Nettles is always muttering about something," said Scarlett. "She's weird. Nothing bad is going to happen to the lake." She hoped she was right. She was certain that Blaze was very close to discovering her magic—she'd

seen sparks coming from her hooves when she'd raced Isabel and Cloud back to the stables. She smiled as she imagined what would happen if one day she just took off into the air and swooped over everyone's heads. Yes, flying would definitely be the most awesome power to have!

CHAPTER 4

The following day was Sunday, and students were allowed an extra hour in bed, so Scarlett was not pleased when Layla woke the whole dorm at the usual time, going to the window and flinging back the curtains with an urgent cry. "Oh no! Look at the lake, everyone!"

Sleepily, Scarlett tumbled out of her warm bed and went to the frosty window with the others. Layla pushed the window up so that everyone could see and dislodged a thick layer of snow from the roof above.

"Brrrr," shivered Scarlett as a blast of cold air

stung her face. She slammed the window shut again.

"But the lake!" cried Layla.

"Look at it!" gasped Sophia. "It's completely frozen!"

The lake's surface was as smooth as glass, with swirls of color trapped inside. Even the fountain was a glassy statue, the rainbow-colored water

frozen into towering spirals, with beads of water scattered over the icy lake like bright jewels.

"It's so pretty," breathed Scarlett, looking in awe at the beautiful colors.

"It's a disaster," said Layla, turning pale. "I'm going to check on Dancer right away. Thank goodness we collected water yesterday," she added as she pulled on a pair of jodhpurs. "There's enough for a few days—if we're all very careful." She shot a look at Scarlett.

Scarlett felt guilty but pushed the uncomfortable feeling away. Layla was far too serious about things. She should just lighten up. So what if the lake was frozen? Everything was bound to be fine in a few days.

Scarlett dressed and headed to the stables through the falling snow. She slowed as she passed the lake. Snow was beginning to collect on the surface, thicker than icing on a cake. Scarlett imagined building an igloo and having snowball fights. Was it wrong to be just a teeny bit excited? The freeze wouldn't last long, so why couldn't they enjoy it? Feet crunching through the thick snow, she hurried to the stables.

Blaze was in a lively mood, tickling Scarlett with her red-and-gold tail from the moment she arrived.

"Stop it," Scarlett giggled. "I want to tell you about the lake."

Blaze stood still and frowned. "I'm listening."

"It's froz— Ooooh! Blaze! Stop it!" Scarlett collapsed in giggles as Blaze made a goofy expression.

"Tell me. I'm listening now," said Blaze, serious again, but as Scarlett started speaking, she turned around and tickled her once more.

"It's snowing and the lake is frozen!" yelled

Scarlett, grabbing Blaze's tail. That got her attention. She swung back and stared with wide eyes.

"I know. It's awful." Scarlett lowered her voice. "But it's not as if you don't have anything to drink. There's enough stored water to last for a while. I bet this cold weather will end soon, so we'd better make the most of it. Do you want to play in the snow?"

"That sounds fun," Blaze agreed eagerly.

Most people had decided to stay in the warm stables with their unicorns, braiding their manes, weaving friendship bracelets, and discussing the big freeze. Even Isabel wanted to stay out of the cold, having a contest with Olivia and Sophia as to who could braid the most ribbons into their unicorns' tails. Scarlett and Blaze threaded their way among the chattering students, who were

busy swapping colored ribbons and bottles of glittery hoof polish, to reach the door.

Outside at last, Blaze's breath puffed icy white clouds as she waited for Scarlett to climb on her back. "Look at me!" she snorted. "I'm smoking like a dragon!"

"Me too!" huffed Scarlett, pursing her lips so that her breath came out in rings. "There's enough snow to build an igloo or a snow unicorn."

"Let's have a snowball fight first!" Blaze lifted her hooves high as she waded through the snow. Veering away from the lake, she headed toward the fields and woods.

"Faster!" Scarlett cried.

Blaze snorted as she sped up, her mane and tail flying out behind her. The cold air stung Scarlett's cheeks and blew her hair into her face. She swiped it away, yelling, "Brake!" as the woods came nearer.

Blaze leaned back, digging her hooves into the snow and trying to stop. The icy snow hissed under her hooves, and a rainbow-colored cloud of steam rose up, enveloping Scarlett.

"What just happened?" Scarlett gasped, snowball fight forgotten.

Blaze lifted a hoof and shook it, sending multicolored water droplets spinning away. "The snow under my hooves is melting!" she said.

"Oh." Scarlett was disappointed. She'd hoped that the freeze would last for a bit longer. She heard a shout and turned to see a floppy-haired boy and a unicorn with an electric-blue mane and tail chasing after them.

"Billy!"

Billy's unicorn, Lightning, wasn't as sure-footed in the snow as Blaze. His legs seemed to go in several directions at once.

"Let's meet them halfway," Scarlett suggested.

"Show them how it's done," added Blaze cheekily.

She trotted toward Lightning, lifting her hooves high, dancing through the snow and then speeding

up and skating in a swerve, leaving a long wiggly trail behind her on the snowy ground.

"Show-offs!" Billy called.

"That's just for warm-ups," Scarlett called back. "Blaze," she whispered, "can you do something else, like a jump?"

Blaze sped up, then leaped in the air, kicking out her legs and swishing her tail. Scarlett whooped. It felt as if they were flying! As she landed, the snow hissed under Blaze's hooves again, and a fiery shower of bright-orange sparks flew into the air along with rainbow-colored steam clouds.

"Whoa!" gasped Billy. "What's happening?"

"I don't know," said Blaze in surprise.

Scarlett caught an overwhelming scent of burnt sugar, and her eyes widened. "Blaze! I know what's going on! You've just discovered your magic power!"

CHAPTER 5

Blaze trembled with excitement. "Oh, Scarlett! It is magic! I can feel it tingling through me." She stared at her hooves. "Did you see the sparks? I was sure I was going to be a flying unicorn, but I think I have fire magic instead!"

"Fire magic? Are you sure?" For a moment, when they were spinning around so fast in the air, Scarlett had thought that Blaze had taken off and was flying. She felt a rush of disappointment.

"Yes!" said Blaze. "I think that's why the snow is melting under my hooves."

"Fire magic!" Billy gave Scarlett and Blaze an

envious look. "Lucky! We're hoping for fire magic, aren't we, Lightning?"

Lightning nodded vigorously. "My dad does fire magic. It was so much fun when I was little. He used to toast sky berries and make amazing displays of colored sparks. Show us your flames again, Blaze."

"Yes, try again!" urged Scarlett, thinking Billy and Lightning were right—maybe fire magic would be fun.

Blaze stamped a front hoof again. There was a loud crack. Tiny red and gold flames flickered up.

"You're doing it, Blaze! You're brilliant!" encouraged Scarlett. Blaze stamped again, harder. Sparks flew up from her hooves, and little pools of hissing water formed wherever they landed.

Lightning looked wistful. "I wish we had some sky berries to toast."

"We could look for toffee nuts in the woods and

toast those," said Scarlett eagerly. She pointed to a tall tree on the edge of the forest. "That looks like a toffee tree."

Blaze stared at the tree intently and then stamped. *CRACK!* A flame arched from her hoof, speeding toward the toffee nuts hanging from the branches. *POP!* It hit the tree. Several nuts flared a warm, glowing red, then fell to the ground.

"Whoa!" Billy's mouth fell open.

"Brilliant!" shouted Scarlett, hugging Blaze. She jumped down and took off her scarf to catch another cluster of toasted nuts as they fell from the tree. There was a rich smell of warm toffee. "You're amazing, Blaze!"

The nuts glowed brightly, then turned a dull purple in a puff of brown-colored smoke. They smelled delicious. As Scarlett and Billy stuffed the toasted nuts into their mouths, a haughty voice rang out.

"Don't you know it's dangerous to play with fire?" No one had heard Valentina approaching on Golden Briar. She halted at the edge of the trees.

Scarlett rolled her eyes. "Blaze is doing just fine. Go away."

Valentina's face turned sour. "I'll tell. My parents are school directors, you know."

"Really, you should have said sooner," Billy muttered, making Scarlett giggle.

Valentina urged Golden Briar forward. "Your unicorn shouldn't be playing with fire when she's only just discovered her powers. Stop it right now!" she commanded.

Blaze's eyes glinted and she stamped down hard. Fire curled from her hoof, running around Golden Briar in a circle, leaving a trail of melted snow. Golden Briar shied backward, his hooves slipping and spraying slush everywhere.

"Eeek!" Valentina shrieked. "We're getting wet!"

"How can fire make you wet?" asked Blaze innocently, conjuring up more flames to blast the snow-covered branches. The melting snow created hissing streams of water that rained down on Valentina and Golden Briar.

Valentina was purple with fury. "Stop it at once, you horrible thing."

"I'm trying," said Blaze, blasting more snow. "Help me, Valentina. I can't control my magic."

Golden Briar snorted angrily and dashed away from the trees, sliding in the slushy ice. He didn't stop until he was far in the distance. Scarlett could barely stand up straight from laughing so much. Each time she managed to stop, Billy and Lightning laughed so hard they set her off again.

Billy clutched his stomach. "That was brilliant!" he chortled. "Valentina's silly. I think it's great that Blaze can melt the snow. What should we do next, Blaze?"

"Let's play a game!" said Blaze. "I'm bursting with energy. It must be the magic."

Scarlett and Billy collected a pine cone and sticks, and Blaze marked out two goals, melting lines in the snow with her fire magic, for a game of hockey. Once the game started, she cheated like mad, using fire to create multicolored puddles and tall clouds of rainbow mist to stop Billy and Lightning from reaching their goal.

"Twenty-seven goals to three," whooped Scarlett. "We won!"

"You and Blaze win at cheating," laughed Billy.

"You're just a sore loser!" teased Scarlett.

"Whatever. I'm hungry now," said Billy. "Let's

go and get lunch." He grinned at her. "I would definitely have won if you hadn't cheated."

Scarlett and Billy rode back toward the stables, teasing each other. They were almost there when Layla and Dancer came over. Layla was walking beside Dancer, her arm around his neck.

"Congratulations," Layla said shyly. "I saw Blaze making flames. She's found her magical power, then?"

"Yes, isn't it brilliant?" said Scarlett.

"Brilliant," Layla agreed. "You looked like you were having lots of fun. Have you told Ms. Rosemary?"

Ms. Rosemary was their advisor. She also taught Unicorn Care, and all students had to tell her when their unicorns discovered their magic power.

"Not yet," said Scarlett.

"You should tell her as soon as possible," said

Layla. "And be careful," she added seriously. "Blaze should practice lots, especially with fire magic. It's really powerful. You could both get hurt."

Scarlett sighed. Why did Layla have to be so boring all the time? "We'll be fine," she said airily. "Race you back to the stables, Billy?"

"See you there! Go, Lightning!" Billy shouted as Lightning set off.

Scarlett whooped as Blaze raced after them at a flat-out gallop.

CHAPTER 6

Lunch was hot soup with crusty bread straight from the oven. Scarlett was hungry! As she ate, she told Isabel everything that had happened.

"I can't believe I stayed in the stables and didn't see it," groaned Isabel. "You're so lucky. Fire magic sounds awesome."

"It really is." Scarlett grinned, remembering the way Blaze had soaked Valentina and Golden Briar with snow from the trees. "We can go out together later, and I'll show you."

But when they returned to the stables after lunch, the temperature had dropped further, and neither of them wanted to go back outside. They decided to groom their unicorns in the walkway instead, but Cloud was thirsty, and the water in the troughs had frozen solid again.

"It's freezing as soon as it leaves the spout," said Cloud.

Scarlett was worried. How would the unicorns get enough to drink?

"Can Blaze use her magic to thaw it?" asked Isabel.

Scarlett grinned with relief. "Brilliant idea. What do you think, Blaze? Do you want to show Isabel your magic?"

Blaze nodded eagerly. It wasn't just Isabel and Cloud who were looking. The other students and unicorns nearby were also watching curiously.

"Stand back," Scarlett said grandly. "Give Blaze some room."

"I don't think you should do this, Scarlett," Layla said anxiously. "The books I've been reading say you need to be extra careful with fire magic."

Scarlett ignored her and beat a drumroll on the stable door with her hands. Blaze bowed to the ground as if she was performing. Then, slowly, with lots of show, she pointed her spiraled horn at the main water trough. A flurry of red and gold sparks flew out and landed on the ice, melting it with a loud hiss.

Everyone clapped loudly.

Blaze hadn't finished. She stamped her hoof again and again. The sparks came faster, crackling brightly and warming the water until it began to steam rainbow colors.

"It's like fireworks," squealed Isabel.

Scarlett was so happy, she thought she might burst. "Fire magic's the best," she said, slinging

an arm around Blaze's neck and hugging her. "And you're my best friend."

"Best friends forever," Blaze agreed, nuzzling her hair. She stamped her hooves one after the other playfully. *Whoosh! Whoosh!* A stream of orange and gold sparks flew up in the air. Scarlett giggled as they cascaded everywhere, and everyone else clapped. Blaze stamped harder, loving all the attention, until a hay bale by the storeroom burst into flames!

Valentina was near the storeroom, fetching some hoof polish. "Fire!" she screamed. Valentina's friends Delia and Jacinta shrieked loudly and ran for the door. Valentina barged past them, shoving Delia into Jacinta. Everyone else ran to help their unicorns escape.

Valentina reached the stable door to find the way out blocked by a tall, regal unicorn. He drew himself up to his full height and glared down at her. He was a magnificent creature with a golden

mane and tail and gold swirls on his snowy-white coat.

"Sage!" whispered Scarlett in dismay. Now they were in trouble. Sage was Ms. Primrose's unicorn. He was distantly descended from the first unicorn who'd ever lived on Unicorn Island.

"Get water!" Sage ordered. The students grabbed buckets and threw water from the main drinking trough over the burning hay bale. The fire hissed and spat, the dying flames turning into smoke that made everyone cough.

Scarlett had never seen Sage angry, but now his nostrils flared and his voice was icy. "That was exceptionally irresponsible, Blaze! Magic should be treated with great respect. You will not use magic again until you have taken some lessons with me on how to conduct yourself when using your powers. And you . . ." His gaze fell on Scarlett. "You should have told Ms. Rosemary that Blaze

had discovered her magic instead of encouraging her foolish behavior. Magic is not a party trick. The sooner you learn that lesson, the better!"

Blaze stared at the floor. Scarlett's red face matched Blaze's with embarrassment.

Valentina sniggered, but Sage turned to her next. "I'm surprised at you, Valentina. I thought you'd have tried to help your unicorn and friends to escape the fire instead of pushing them out of the way."

Valentina's mouth opened, but Sage fixed her with a steely glare, and she snapped it shut again.

Sage nodded at Blaze. "Clean up this mess and then meet me by the lake." He stomped away.

Scarlett and Blaze set to work, silent for once.

"That's not fair," said Isabel, when Sage was out of hearing. "You shouldn't have to do lessons on our day off."

"I think it serves you right," Valentina said.

Scarlett glared at her, but part of her did feel guilty—setting the hay bale on fire had been dangerous—so she didn't say anything back.

"I hope Sage doesn't make us work outside for too long," she whispered as she and Blaze headed to the lake after cleaning up. "It's so cold."

"You don't have to come," said Blaze. "You could go back inside."

Tempted as she was to take Blaze up on her offer, Scarlett knew it wouldn't be fair. The accident in the stable was her fault too. "No, we're in this together," she replied.

★

Sage's lesson on using magic was difficult. He expected perfection and made Blaze practice over and over again to get things right. Sage put Scarlett to work too, making her fetch and carry things for Blaze to heat and set fire to. She also had to run for the odd bucket of water when Blaze lost control and her fires were too big. She thought longingly of the lounge with its comfy sofas and crackling log fire. By the end of the afternoon, Scarlett and Blaze were exhausted, but Sage seemed satisfied with Blaze's progress.

"Well done. You've worked hard and are beginning to get more control over your power," he said. "Meet me here first thing tomorrow morning after breakfast. I have a job for you."

Scarlett's heart plummeted. "It's jumping tomorrow morning with Ms. Tulip. Could we come later?"

"No. Tomorrow morning, first thing," said Sage firmly. "This task is much more important than a jumping lesson."

"What's the task?" asked Scarlett, but Sage walked away without answering. Scarlett sighed. She had a horrible feeling that the job was going to involve lots more hard work!

CHAPTER 7

Early the next morning, Scarlett arrived, shivering, at the stables. She knew at once from the chatter among the unicorns that something was wrong.

"What's up?" she asked.

"It's so cold that even the stored lake water is beginning to freeze," Blaze said.

Scarlett peered into the heated containers. A thin crust of pink, yellow, and blue ice crystals had formed on the surface of the water inside. They sparkled prettily in the early-morning sunlight streaming through the doors. Scarlett felt a

shiver of fear. Why weren't the heated containers stopping the water from freezing? Had someone tampered with them or put a spell on them and also the lake? But who would do such a terrible thing? Everyone knew how important the waters of Sparkle Lake were to the survival of the island. Scarlett shook the thoughts away. Surely no one from Unicorn Island would be mean enough to freeze the lake on purpose?

Pulling off a glove, she broke up the ice crystals so the unicorns could have a drink, then she and Blaze went to the lake.

Sage was waiting there for them. "This cold snap is getting worse," he said. "Blaze, you are the only unicorn at the school with fire magic. I want you to try to thaw Sparkle Lake. It is a huge task and you may not succeed, but this will be good practice for you and your new power, and you may be able to thaw the lake enough for

the unicorns to drink fresh lake water today. If Sparkle Lake remains frozen, then Ms. Primrose will be forced to close the school."

Scarlett exchanged a worried look with Blaze. She didn't want the school to shut down.

"Scarlett, you can help Blaze by encouraging her. When a unicorn feels loved and confident, their magic becomes stronger," Sage said. "Stay off the ice so you don't fall through it as it melts. Work slowly, starting at the edge, or you'll lose control. Begin!"

Scarlett fell silent as Blaze, watched by Sage, started on the enormous task. Sage had taught Blaze two ways to use her fire magic. She could either stamp a hoof or she could breathe gently onto an object.

Blaze was good at fire making. Each time she stamped on the ice, a red-gold flame flared from her hoof, making the ice crackle and hiss as it

slowly melted. She made it look easy, but Scarlett could see her muscles trembling with effort.

"Come on, Blaze, we can do this," she urged, rubbing her neck.

Many tries later, Blaze managed to create a sliver of water in the ice. It didn't seem like much to Scarlett, especially for all the effort involved, but Sage was delighted.

"It's a good start," he told Blaze. "I must leave you now and contact all the fire unicorns on the

island to ask them for help. Keep up the good work, and be careful." He galloped away.

Scarlett groaned. "This is so boring. Look, there's Isabel and Cloud. Shall we take a break now that Sage has gone? Hey, Isabel. Over here!"

"What are you doing?" asked Isabel, riding Cloud onto the ice.

As Scarlett explained the task Blaze had been given, Isabel's eyes widened. "Can we watch?"

Spurred on by an audience, Blaze lifted her neck and stamped a hoof. A flame arched over Isabel and Cloud, falling at the far side of the lake. A chunk of the ice melted in one try.

"Woo-hoo!" cheered Isabel, and Cloud whinnied loudly.

"Naughty Blaze!" chuckled Scarlett. "You're supposed to be doing a tiny bit at a time."

"This is more fun, though!" Blaze answered. "I bet I could melt the fountain if I tried."

"Ooh, this I have to see," Isabel told Cloud. "Let's get closer."

Blaze whispered to Scarlett, "I'm going to send an arch of fire over Cloud and Isabel and melt the fountain right in front of them."

Scarlett clapped with delight. "Wicked! Go, Blaze!"

Cloud was about to skate over to the fountain when a voice shouted out, "Wait!"

They turned to see Layla hurrying over to the edge of the lake. "You should keep off the ice while Blaze is melting it," she warned Isabel.

Scarlett rolled her eyes at Isabel. Why was Layla being such a pain? It was only a bit of fun. She and Blaze might die of boredom from the huge task they'd been given if they didn't take a break.

Blaze took a deep breath and focused on the frozen fountain. Then she stamped her hoof. *CRACK!* An enormous ball of fire, like a tiny sun,

exploded from Blaze's hoof and arched in the air. Sparking brightly, it landed right in front of Cloud and Isabel, encircling them in a ring of small flames. The ice melted, leaving Isabel and Cloud stranded on a thin shard of floating ice. Isabel yelled, but her panicked words were silenced as the shard tilted and tipped them straight into the freezing water!

CHAPTER 8

"Isabel!" Scarlett screamed. She leaped onto Blaze's back, and they galloped toward the hole.

Cloud, head high, nostrils flaring, was struggling in the water.

"Swim, Cloud!" shouted Isabel, hanging tightly to her mane.

Blaze stopped at the edge of the ice. Scarlett slid from her back, dodging the cracks running across the ice.

"Get back!" Suddenly Layla was at Scarlett's side. "Move Blaze back before she cracks the ice even more."

Slithering and slipping on the glassy surface, Blaze backed away. Scarlett copied Layla as she lay down on her tummy. The shining surface beneath them shivered and groaned. Scarlett held her breath, ignoring the cold burn of the ice seeping through her clothes.

"Here," called Layla, stretching out her hand to Isabel.

Isabel, eyes wide, hung over Cloud's neck. Her fingertips couldn't quite reach Layla's. Scarlett, who was taller, stretched out her hand, but Isabel still couldn't grasp it.

"Stretch!" shouted Scarlett, every muscle in her arm screaming with effort as she tried to grab Isabel's hand. "And a bit more!"

With superhuman effort, Isabel stretched out her arm until her fingers caught hold of Scarlett's.

Scarlett pulled, but she didn't have the strength

to help Isabel and Cloud out of the water. All she achieved was to make the ice hole bigger!

She felt a tug on her hoodie. Layla!

"Hold tight," Layla gasped.

Scarlett gritted her teeth and hung on to Isabel. The ice creaked as it broke away. Then suddenly, Layla gave an extra-hard tug. Scarlett slid backward, pulling a dripping Isabel with her, and Cloud scrambled from the water after her. They landed on the ice. Layla and Blaze dragged them clear of the hole, and Cloud scrabbled to her feet.

Fear brightened Blaze's eyes. "I'm so sorry."

"It's okay," said Isabel, through chattering teeth.

It wasn't okay, though. Seeing Isabel's eyes, large as moons, and Cloud shivering next to her, Scarlett felt terrible. This was as much her fault as Blaze's. "I'm to blame too," she said, hugging Isabel to warm her up. "I should have listened to Layla. I shouldn't have encouraged Blaze."

"That was so scary." Blaze was trembling. "I didn't know the strength of my magic. Sage was right. I need to be much more careful."

"Don't worry. It's fine." Isabel gave Scarlett a shaky smile.

"You and Cloud should get back to the stable and dry off before you both catch a chill," said Layla.

Scarlett swallowed back a small burst of anger. Isabel didn't need Layla to tell her that. With a tight knot in her chest, Scarlett watched Isabel and Cloud ride away. She knew that, somehow, she had to make it up to her best friend.

"I don't believe it!" said Blaze. "The lake has frozen over again already. Look!"

"That's impossible!" Scarlett turned. Blaze was right. "That can't have happened unless . . . unless . . . " Her eyes widened. "Maybe the lake has frozen over because someone has put a spell on it?"

Blaze looked shocked, but Layla nodded. "I've read about freezing spells."

"Why would anyone try to freeze the lake?" asked Blaze.

"I don't know," admitted Scarlett. "But think about it. Ms. Nettles said the lake would never freeze over and it has, and Ava thought she heard Ms. Nettles muttering about a spell."

"I bet you're right," said Blaze. "But if there is a spell, there's no point trying to thaw it because it will just refreeze. So what should we do?"

Scarlett hesitated. "I'm not sure. Let's go back to the stables for now."

At the stables, Layla went to check on her unicorn, Dancer. Scarlett brought Blaze a bucket of sky berries, having picked out the biggest, juiciest ones. "Here, these are for you," she said.

"I'm not hungry." Blaze hung her head. "I still feel awful about what happened at the lake."

"I know, but you need to keep your strength up," insisted Scarlett. She held out a sky berry. "Go on, just eat one. Please."

Blaze took the berry reluctantly.

"Eat another," Scarlett encouraged, holding out a second berry.

Isabel looked into Blaze's stall. "Cloud's dry now, and I'm going back to the dorm to get warm. Are you coming?"

Scarlett was torn, wanting to be with both of her friends.

"Blaze doesn't look too happy," whispered

Isabel, noticing. "I'll be fine on my own. You stay here and feed her."

"Thanks, Isabel. You're a wonderful best friend. I'm really sorry about what happened," Scarlett said gratefully.

Isabel grinned. "It was my fault too. I should have kept off the ice. See you later."

Scarlett patiently fed Blaze the whole bucket of sky berries before she went back inside. She pushed aside her guilt over Isabel and Cloud as she thought about the lake. Had someone put a spell on it? A plan started to form in Scarlett's head. If she and Blaze could break the spell and stop the school from closing, everyone would be so pleased. But how would they do it?

The library, Scarlett thought. *It's bound to have a book that could help!*

★

It was warm indoors, and Scarlett's fingers tingled pleasantly as she hurried along the corridors to the library. She opened the heavy door. In the middle of the room, the librarian's desk was shaped like an enormous book, with a colorful spine and gold lettering.

"Can I help you, dear?" asked Ms. Tansy, the librarian. She blinked at Scarlett through her yellow-rimmed, flower-shaped glasses.

"I'd like a book on spells, please," said Scarlett.

Ms. Tansy beamed. "We have plenty of those! The section you need is over there on the right, next to the History of Unicorn Magic."

Scarlett's feet sank into the thick carpet as she crossed the library. When she reached the section Ms. Tansy had pointed out, she stopped abruptly. The spells section took up a whole wall! Now what was she going to do? She groaned. If she wanted to make it up to Isabel and Cloud, she'd better get reading!

CHAPTER 9

An hour later, Scarlett rubbed her eyes. Closing the book in her lap, she tucked it under her arm, then climbed the ladder for the umpteenth time to the top shelf. She didn't know how many books she had read, but none of them had said anything about removing a freezing spell.

Replacing the book, Scarlett reached for its neighbor, but someone else got there first.

"Layla!" Scarlett put a hand on the book. "I really need this. Can I borrow it first?"

"Why don't we look together?" said Layla.

"I spend a lot of time in here, reading about unicorns."

Scarlett had wanted to solve the problem of the lake by herself, to make it up to Isabel and to prove to everyone, particularly Layla, that she could be serious when it mattered. But Layla was clever and she clearly meant well, even though she could be incredibly annoying. Maybe she could help her. "Okay, let's work together," Scarlett said. She explained her suspicion about the freezing spell.

It hardly took Layla any time at all to work out which book they needed. Minutes later, they were sitting on purple cushions with a massive book about seasonal and elemental spells on their knees and their backs to the reading tree—a real tree with multicolored leaves that magically grew in the library. Scarlett couldn't believe how quickly Layla could read, her eyes rapidly skimming over the pages. They found a chapter on freezing spells near the end.

"Breaking a freezing spell sounds really complicated," Scarlett said doubtfully as they read through the chapter. "There are so many different spells and potions you can use."

"And they all need such strange ingredients to work," said Layla. "Wait!" she added. "What's this? It says that any water-freezing spell can be broken if a diamond from the Diamond Glacier in the Frozen Wastelands is placed upon the frozen water."

Scarlett caught her breath. "So if I could get one of those diamonds, I could break the spell on the lake."

"You could, but the Frozen Wastelands are miles away," Layla pointed out. "It would take days to get there."

An idea popped into Scarlett's head. "Not if I used the magical map!"

The magical map in the center of the school hall was a miniature model of Unicorn Island. It had tiny mountains, valleys, ice, sea, and even Unicorn Academy, complete with a lake and a fountain. The map was extremely powerful and could take you anywhere on the island if you just touched the place you wanted to go.

"But you can only use the map with Ms. Primrose's permission," Layla reminded her. "And she only lets people use it in emergencies."

"This is definitely an emergency. I'm going to ask her right now," said Scarlett, jumping to her feet. She thought about asking Layla if she'd go with her but quickly changed her mind. Layla wasn't brave enough for this adventure.

"Will you really go to the Wastelands if Ms. Primrose says you can use the map?" Layla asked.

Scarlett nodded. "I have to."

Layla twisted her braid around her hand in a thick coil. "I'd better come with you. We should ask Blaze and Dancer along too."

"Really? You'll come with me?" said Scarlett.

Layla didn't look totally sure, but she squared her shoulders. "Absolutely."

Scarlett's eyes sparkled. "Thanks! Let's go and see Ms. Primrose."

But when they knocked on the head teacher's door, there was no answer.

Layla looked relieved. "Oh, well, I suppose we'll just have to wait until Ms. Primrose comes back."

"No!" said Scarlett. "I'm sure Ms. Primrose won't mind us using the map without asking. After all, if we're right about the spell, we could save the whole island by getting this diamond!"

"I really don't think we should go without checking with her first," said Layla doubtfully.

"You can stay here if you want." Scarlett's mouth set in a determined line. "I'm going."

"But you can't go on your own! The Wastelands are the coldest, bleakest part of the island. There's nothing there except steep glaciers and dangerous man-eating bears." Layla shivered. "No, if you're going, then I'm going too!"

Scarlett was surprised but didn't want to waste any more time talking about it. "Okay, let's go!"

They ran to the stables and explained their plan to Blaze and to Dancer—Layla's small, slightly shaggy blue-and-silver unicorn. Both unicorns were very excited when they heard the plan and were eager to race to the hall. When they stepped inside the grand room, cool winter sunlight was shining through the domed glass roof, making rainbow patterns on the floor. In the center of the room was the magical map of the island, showing the snowy mountains, green valleys, and golden beaches.

As the girls and unicorns approached the map, the force field protecting the map glimmered more brightly. Goose bumps skittered along Scarlett's arms. The magical field hummed musically. Would it let them through? Scarlett and Blaze walked through the shimmering barrier, their skin sparkling gold. Layla and Dancer followed. There was a bright flash, and the force field vanished.

"Look," breathed Scarlett, leaning over the mini lake and fountain. "Frozen solid just like the real ones." Her eyes searched the map. "That's where we have to go," she said, pointing to a glacier in the Frozen Wastelands in the north. It had steep sides leading up to a tall, icy crown. Frozen beneath the surface of the crown, hundreds of diamonds seemed to sparkle.

"Hold my hand," Scarlett said to Layla, who was suddenly looking very anxious. "We have to

touch the map and then it will take us where we want to go. My sisters told me that."

Excitement rushed through Scarlett as she reached out and touched the glacier. Immediately, an icy wind whipped around them, whisking her off her feet. Layla's hand was torn from hers as they spun around. Lights sparked, cold air pinched Scarlett's cheeks and nose. Then she was falling. . . .

CHAPTER 10

Scarlett clung to Blaze's mane as they plummeted downward. A heap of soft snow cushioned their fall. Scarlett jumped to her feet, shaking the snow crystals from her blond hair. Blaze leaped up too, and they both looked around. They were at the foot of the steep glacier. Scarlett's heart sank. The diamonds were at the top of the glacier at the crown. They were going to have to climb!

There was a whizzing sound, reminding Scarlett of the buzz of a fly, and something plopped into the snow at her feet. Instinctively, she snatched it up, but before she could look to see what it was,

Dancer came thudding down through the air, skidding into Blaze and sending her flying.

"Sorry!" Layla's eyes were huge as she hung on tight to Dancer until he finally stopped rocketing around. "What do you have, Scarlett?"

"I don't know." Scarlett held out her palm, revealing a toy building, like a tiny model. It looked familiar, but it took several seconds to work out why. "It's Unicorn Academy," she said in surprise. "Is it yours, Layla? It's definitely not mine."

Layla shook her head. "It's not mine either. Where did you find it?"

"It found me!" Scarlett studied the toy closely. She was impressed with how lifelike it was. But why had it just appeared?

"What's that noise?" Layla said suddenly.

Scarlett could hear it too—a fearful growl that made the hairs on the back of her neck stand up. It sounded like . . .

"A saber-toothed polar bear!" she cried as she turned and saw a giant bear behind them. She shoved the little model of the school into her pocket. The white monster bear was ten times bigger than Blaze. Its tiny eyes burned with fury as it reared up on its hind legs. Its long claws were sharper than knives. Opening its cavelike mouth, it roared, showing yellowing razor-sharp teeth.

Layla screamed.

"Gallop!" cried Scarlett, vaulting onto Blaze's back. Her legs were like jelly as Blaze took off. All she could think of was the polar bear's teeth and deadly claws.

Blaze stormed up the side of the glacier, with Dancer right beside her. Scarlett's heartbeat matched the thud of Blaze's hooves as they galloped. The ground behind them shook as the polar bear gave chase.

"Faster!" urged Scarlett. Her hands gripped Blaze's mane as she leaned forward, willing her on.

The polar bear was close behind them. Every time it roared, it gave off a blast of hot breath that stank like rotting fish. Blaze and Dancer galloped bravely, but their hooves were slipping and sliding as they climbed the glacier. The saber-toothed bear was gaining on them. There was no way they could outrun it, and there was nowhere to

hide. Scarlett glanced across at Layla. Filled with terror and looking like she was about to faint, Layla clung to Dancer's neck.

"I need something to fight with!" Scarlett scanned the glacier for sticks or rocks, but there was nothing but ice.

"I can do it!" panted Blaze. "Hold tight, Scarlett. I'll fight this bear with my fire magic."

Blaze skidded on the ice, using the momentum to turn to face the bear. Scarlett gasped, her fingers sinking deeper into Blaze's mane. She felt Blaze tremble, but she kept calm and took a deep breath. *CRACK!* Blaze shot a firebolt from her gold-and-red spiraled horn. The bear roared in surprise and leaped away as the fire landed at its paws.

Scarlett punched the air with her fist. "Go, Blaze!"

"Be careful!" squeaked Layla.

The bear reared up, claws slashing the air, but it looked less confident now. Blaze sent more fireballs spinning its way. This time they hit the bear's paws, and the smell of burning fur filled the air. The bear yelped. Blaze fired another round. Two fireballs singed the bear's ears, and another hit its nose. The bear roared, and then fled back down the glacier away from the fireballs and the two unicorns.

Scarlett, her heart in her mouth, found she couldn't speak for a second.

"Thanks, Blaze," said Layla hoarsely.

Blaze looked delighted. "That'll teach it to attack unicorns!"

Now that the bear had gone, Scarlett began to enjoy the ride to the top of the glacier. She'd never been in the Frozen Wastelands before, and it was a place of strange beauty, with sparkling white snow, pale-blue skies, glittering ice, and jagged mountains. She was so busy enjoying the feeling of being on an adventure, it was a while before she realized that Layla and Dancer had fallen behind. Dancer had stopped and was talking to Layla.

"What's up?" called Scarlett, looking around.

"I . . . I'm scared, Scarlett," said Layla in a trembling voice. "I don't want to be here. I want to go home."

Scarlett blinked in surprise. She'd just been thinking how much fun it was exploring somewhere new.

Layla's eyes filled with tears. "I'm sorry. I'm such a coward."

As Scarlett looked at Layla, she remembered that Layla hadn't seemed happy about the adventure at all, but that she'd still insisted on coming. Scarlett suddenly felt bad, and instead of teasing her, she rode Blaze over to Layla and put a hand on her shoulder. "You're not a coward. Anyone would be scared after being chased by a polar bear. But the bear's gone now, and it's not too far to the top, where the diamonds are."

"I know, but I don't usually ride much at all," Layla said. "And I'm tired."

She was clinging to Dancer's mane, her knees gripping his sides, and Scarlett realized that despite Layla's knowledge about unicorns, she wasn't at all confident on her unicorn's back. It was a really big deal for Layla to agree to come with her. It must have taken a huge amount of courage.

Dancer nuzzled Layla's leg. "I promise I'll look after you, Layla," he told her. "We're almost there. We can't give up now."

Scarlett nodded. "We don't have a choice. We've got to go on, to save Sparkle Lake and all the people, animals, and plants of Unicorn Island."

Layla gritted her teeth. "You're right," she said.

Scarlett smiled at her. "We're going to do this! We're going to save the lake!" As Blaze picked her way up the side of the glacier beside Dancer, Scarlett chatted with Layla, distracting her from the steep, icy climb.

When they finally reached the top, Scarlett fell silent. The crown of the glacier was like a huge glass tabletop, with hundreds of sparkling diamonds just below the frozen surface. Below them, Unicorn Island stretched out far into the distance, every bit as beautiful as the magical map. Scarlett was filled with a mixture of wonder and pride. This was her home. If she could just collect a diamond and take it back to the lake, she would be able to save it.

She lifted her chin. *Nothing's going to stop me!* she thought.

CHAPTER 11

Scarlett dismounted and crouched beside a large pink diamond that shone like the setting sun just beneath the surface of the ice. It was tantalizingly close, but the glacier surface was as hard as iron, and no matter how often Scarlett hit it with the heel of her riding boot, she didn't even make a dent in the ice.

"Let me try. Maybe I can melt it," said Blaze. Standing over the diamond, she stamped down hard. There was a pop, and a ball of fire sizzled across the surface. Blaze stamped harder, sending bigger balls of fire hissing and crackling over the ice, but it remained solid. Blaze breathed gently on it, causing so much steam she almost disappeared from view, but still the ice stayed frozen.

"It's useless," Blaze sighed.

Scarlett could feel uncertainty coursing through Blaze. She stroked her neck. "No, it's not. You can do this, Blaze. You're the only unicorn at the school with fire magic. Even Sage can't do that! If anyone can get this diamond, it's you!"

As she spoke, Blaze lifted her head, her eyes glowing with new confidence. She stamped her hoof, and with an explosive crack, golden-red flames shot from her horn and drilled into the frozen ground. Steam rose in the air, and the ice bubbled and spat as it dissolved.

"Ooh! That's lovely and warm," giggled Scarlett, pulling her glove off and dipping her hand in the water. A moment later, she plucked the sparkling diamond free. Dripping water down Scarlett's arm, the diamond glittered brightly. "I've got it, Blaze! You did it!"

Blaze nuzzled Scarlett. "We did it, but it's not over yet. We've got to get back to the lake. How are we going to do that?"

Squinting into the sinking sun, Scarlett looked at the island. The Frozen Wastelands stretched far into the distance before the landscape gradually softened into the green meadows and blue-gray mountains beyond. Her heart sank. They were miles from home. How were they going to get back?

She saw Dancer, Blaze, and Layla looking at her expectantly. But she didn't have an answer. "We're going to . . . um . . ."

Playing for time, she pushed the diamond deep into her pocket, and as she did, her fingers touched the model of the academy that had mysteriously appeared when they arrived at the Wastelands. Her fingers tingled as they brushed against it, and she pulled it out. It was sparkling and glowing! She stared at it in astonishment.

"Of course!" gasped Layla. "That's how we'll return to school!"

"It is?" Scarlett said uncertainly.

"Yes! It makes sense. The map wouldn't be any use without a way of getting home. Look at how the model's sparkling. It's magic, and I think it's ready to take us back!" She rode Dancer over to Scarlett. "Hold my hand!"

Scarlett vaulted onto Blaze, and the two girls held hands. The little model sparkled brightly.

"We want to return to Unicorn Academy!" Layla said.

A fierce wind sprang up. Scarlett gasped as her hair flew out behind her like a banner, and then she and the others were whisked into the air. Around and around they spun, faster and faster. At first she could see Layla and Dancer spinning beside them. Then everything blurred. She felt herself plummeting down, and then Blaze hit the ground with a thump.

"We're back!" cried Layla in relief.

They were standing in the school gardens. Scarlett's hand was empty. The model had vanished. Scarlett pulled the diamond from her pocket. "Now let's get this to the lake!"

The girls and their unicorns set off toward the lake. Blaze raced like the wind across the grass, speeding past other unicorns and their riders. Scarlett heard shouting and neighs, but she blocked them out. As Blaze skidded to a stop, Scarlett threw the diamond to the center of the lake. It soared through the air. *Plink!* It slid across the ice, leaving a long, thin scratch in its wake. The ice gave a groan, and the whole surface shook. Scarlett heard surprised shouts behind her. There was a loud crack, and the ice shattered into a thousand glittering multicolored pieces. Water oozed over the shards of ice, and bubbles surfaced and popped in little clouds of color.

"What happened?"

"What did you do?"

A babble of voices rose up behind Scarlett and Layla. They turned and saw people running toward them, including the rest of Sapphire dorm. Scarlett waved at Isabel in delight. She couldn't wait to tell her best friend what she had been up to. She knew Isabel and Cloud were going to be thrilled that the lake was saved!

Another voice rang out. It was Ms. Nettles!

"What are you doing?" Ms. Nettles sucked in her thin cheeks, and her glasses rattled furiously. "What is all this shrieking and shouting about?"

Her words were drowned out by the drum of hooves as Sage galloped up from the school with Ms. Primrose on his back.

"The lake!" Sage exclaimed, looking almost lost for words. "You've melted all the ice, Blaze!"

"Yes, she did," Scarlett said. "Well, we both did, but not by using Blaze's fire magic." The words rushed out as Scarlett explained about the freezing spell and about her adventure with Layla to the Frozen Wastelands to get the magic diamond.

"I'm sorry I went on an adventure without you," Scarlett added to Isabel and Cloud. "Everything happened so fast, and Layla wanted to come and help."

"That's okay," said Isabel. "I'm just glad you're all right and that you've saved the island!"

Scarlett couldn't help smiling as her guilt lifted. "Blaze was amazing today! She fought off a saber-toothed polar bear and got the diamond out of the glacier. Layla was fantastic too. She helped me find all the information we needed, and she came with me even though she was afraid, and she got us back to school!"

"I didn't want Scarlett doing something so dangerous on her own," said Layla. Scarlett glanced at her quickly. So that had been Layla's reason for coming—that made her even more brave in Scarlett's eyes.

Scarlett looked at Ms. Primrose. "Are we in trouble for using the map? If we are, please don't blame Layla. It was all my fault. She tried to stop me."

"Yes, you are in trouble," said Ms. Primrose.

"You shouldn't have used the map without my permission. I can see you had the best intentions, but you should never go off like that, especially without telling anyone." Ms. Primrose fixed Scarlett and Layla with a very hard glare. Then her face softened into a smile. "But well done for thawing the lake, all of you. I can see I should be watching Sapphire dorm—this is not the first time one of you has saved the day!"

"Someone must have cast the freezing spell in the first place," said Layla. "We have to find out who it was."

"You can leave that to me, my dear," said Ms. Primrose. "I will give it my urgent attention. But for now, I think a little celebration would be appropriate. You may have a special dinner by the lake. Ms. Nettles, would you kindly arrange for plenty of warm blankets and a big bag of marshmallows? And, Blaze, I think you might have one more small job to do for this evening's celebrations. . . ."

"Yes, Ms. Primrose. Good work, girls, and good work, Blaze and Cloud," said Ms. Nettles, and she even managed a faint smile.

★

A short while later, Scarlett, her friends from Sapphire dorm, and their unicorns all stood by the lake, waiting for Blaze to light a huge stack of wood for a bonfire. Blaze lifted her foot to make a spark, when Isabel suddenly cried, "Scarlett, look! Look at your hair."

"What?" Scarlett tilted her head, and a fiery-red lock of hair fell over her face. Her eyes widened as she held it up to Blaze's mane. The colors were identical. "We've bonded!" Scarlett threw her arms around Blaze's neck. "We've really bonded," she squealed.

"Of course we have. We're best friends forever," cried Blaze, nuzzling Scarlett's neck.

Scarlett's eyes caught Layla's.

"Thank you," Layla said softly, sidling up to her. "You helped me today when we were in the Wastelands. I was so scared."

Scarlett shrugged. "I didn't do anything."

"You did," said Layla. "I was terrified, but you didn't tease me, and you made me feel better."

"It was really brave of you to come along when you don't like riding much," Scarlett said.

"Thanks for coming with me—and helping me in the library before we went."

"Any time," Layla said with a smile.

Scarlett didn't think she'd ever felt happier. She turned to Blaze. "Ready?" she asked.

Blaze stamped her hoof. It cracked on the ground, and the bonfire flared into life with a *whoosh*.

Scarlett reached for a bag of pink and white sweets. "Anyone for marshmallows?" she called. "I hear they're very nice toasted!"

Scarlett shared the marshmallows as the other girls crowded around her, warmed by the orange, gold, and red flames that flickered and danced, lighting up the dark blue sky.

When the sky berries that unicorns
need to survive disappear,
it's up to Ava and Star to find them
before every unicorn's magic starts to fade.

Read on for a peek at the next book
in the Unicorn Academy series!

CHAPTER 1

"Star, wake up," whispered Ava.

Star was asleep in her stable. She looked so sweet, with her eyes shut tight and her yellow-and-purple mane curling over her white coat. Ava smoothed a lilac curl that was sticking up between Star's spiraled gold-and-purple horn.

"Ava?" Star's eyes snapped open and she scrambled to her hooves. "It's early, even for you. Is something wrong?"

Ava grinned. "No, everything's fine. I'm just excited! Last night the teachers told us we're going on a scavenger hunt this morning instead

of lessons. We've got to collect things from around the school grounds in teams!"

Star pricked up her ears. "That sounds fun!"

Ava nodded. "I woke up thinking about it, and when I looked out the window, I saw something I had to show you. Come with me!"

Blinking and yawning, Star followed Ava through the stable of sleeping unicorns to the door.

Ava stopped. "Close your eyes."

Star obediently shut her eyes. Ava felt her heart swell with happiness as she realized how much her unicorn trusted her. Putting her hand on Star's warm neck, she guided her outside.

"You can open them now," she whispered. "Look!"

"Wow!" Star blinked. A ball of sunshine was visible on the horizon. As it rose, filling the gap between two mountains, the dark sky rippled with orange, pink, and gold.

"Doesn't the school look beautiful?" said Ava. Across the lawn, the marble walls and glass windows of Unicorn Academy glowed in the sunrise, and in the distance the multicolored water of Sparkle Lake glittered and shone.

"It's the best sunrise I've seen in ages," said Star.

Ava smiled. "I had to share it with you. Spring's coming, Star. I can smell it in the air! Shall we plant my new seedlings before I have to go for breakfast?"

"Good plan!" said Star eagerly. "I'll dig the holes."

"That would be brilliant." Ava kissed her unicorn on the purple star on her forehead. "I love having you as my unicorn. I can't imagine being partnered with a unicorn who didn't like gardening!"

"And I can't imagine being partnered with a girl who didn't like nature!" said Star, her warm breath tickling Ava and making her giggle.

Ava and Star had been paired together in January, three months ago, when they'd both started at Unicorn Academy. Ava still found it hard to believe that she was really here, training to become a guardian of wonderful Unicorn Island.

The island was nourished by magical waters that flowed up from the center of the earth and out through the fountain in Sparkle Lake. Rivers carried the precious water around the land so that it helped all the people, animals, and plants on Unicorn Island to flourish.

Students usually spent a year at Unicorn Academy when they were ten, but sometimes they stayed longer if their unicorn needed more time to discover their magic power or if they hadn't yet bonded with their unicorn. Bonding was the highest form of friendship, and when it happened, a lock of the student's hair would turn the same color as their unicorn's mane. Ava couldn't help feeling a little surprised she and Star hadn't bonded already.

"Do you think Ms. Primrose paired us together because we both love plants and nature?" asked Star.

★ ★ ★

"Maybe," said Ava. "Or maybe there was another reason. You never know with Ms. Primrose."

Ms. Primrose was the wise head teacher who had been in charge of the academy for many years. She was strict, but she could also be very kind.

"Well, whatever her reason, I'm glad she did," said Star. "I wonder when I'll find out what my magic power is and when we'll bond."

Ava felt a clench in her stomach. Two of the girls from Sapphire dorm had already bonded with their unicorns. Ava couldn't help but worry that she was doing something wrong. She knew a lot about plants and animals, but she wasn't very good at reading and writing. What if Star never found her magic power and they never bonded because she wasn't clever enough to help her? That would be awful!

Star nudged her. "Should we get your plants from the greenhouse?"

Ava squashed her growing anxiety. “Aren’t you forgetting something?” she said. “You haven’t had any breakfast yet!”

Star burst out laughing. “Silly me, I’m getting as forgetful as you, Ava!”

“Impossible!” Ava chuckled.

She and Star went back inside the stables. Ava found a bucket and went to fill it with sky berries. But when she lifted the lid of the feed bin, she blinked in surprise.

“It’s almost empty!” she said to Star, who was watching from the doorway. She checked the other feed bins. “They all are.”

“What? They

can't be. The gardeners fill the bins with berries every day," said Star.

Sky berries grew on the mountain slopes behind the school. Not only were they the unicorns' favorite food, but they were full of the vitamins they needed to stay healthy and helped keep the unicorns' magic strong.

Star came over to check, but as she put her nose into a feed bin, she knocked it over. The remaining berries spilled onto the floor.

"Star!" exclaimed Ava.

"Whoops!" said Star, nudging the berries into a pile with her muzzle. "I'm sorry, Ava."

"Don't worry." Ava scooped them up and put them back into the bin. She adored Star, but sometimes she wished she weren't quite so clumsy. "There are only enough berries for the unicorns to have breakfast. I'd better tell Ms. Rosemary." Ms. Rosemary, the Care of Unicorns teacher, was

in charge of the stables. "Now, eat up," she said, filling Star's bucket with berries.

Star gobbled up her berries. As she finished her last mouthful, she gave Ava a hopeful look. "Is there still time to plant your new seedlings before breakfast?"

"If we're quick," said Ava.

First Ava and Star went to the potting shed to collect their gardening tools, then to the greenhouse for Ava's plants. Between them they carried everything to Ava's small patch of garden.

The spring earth was soft and easy to dig. Star made the holes, while Ava rescued the worms that got dug up, carefully moving them to a new home. Then Ava placed each seedling into a hole and patted earth around it. Star leaned over her shoulder. The last seedling was smaller than the rest. Star accidently nudged it with her nose and it fell over.

Puff! A tiny spark flickered next to the plant.

"Oh!" exclaimed Ava.

"Sorry, I was being clumsy again," said Star anxiously. "I didn't do any damage, did I?"

"I meant the spark." Ava sniffed the air. "And what's that sweet smell?"

"What smell?" Star looked mystified.

"It's gone now, but it smelled like . . ." Ava shook her head. "Nothing, I probably imagined it. For a second I thought you were getting your magic, though. Wouldn't it be brilliant if you had plant magic? Imagine what fun we could have."

Every unicorn had a special type of magic. In Sapphire dorm, Sophia's unicorn had light magic and Scarlett's unicorn had fire magic.

Star stared at Ava. "Plant magic is very powerful. I'm much too clumsy to have something that special."

"Being clumsy doesn't matter. I bet you could have plant magic!" Ava dusted the dirt from her hands and then stroked Star's forehead. "Why don't you try again?"

Star dipped her head and blew on the ground. Nothing happened. She gently touched the row of seedlings with her nose, taking extra care not to knock them over.

"Nothing," she said sadly. "They're exactly the same size. I knew I wouldn't have plant magic."

"You still might!" Ava hugged her tightly. "And anyway, I love you just the way you are, whatever magic you end up having."

Star whinnied happily.

Just then there was the sound of someone approaching at a fast gallop. Ava looked around and saw her best friend, Sophia, racing up to them on her handsome unicorn, Rainbow.

"Sophia! You look like you're in a hurry!" exclaimed Ava.

"I am," panted Sophia, her dark curls bouncing on her shoulders as Rainbow halted. "You need to come with me. Ms. Rosemary wants us all to meet at Sparkle Lake. We're about to start the scavenger hunt!"

"But what about breakfast?" said Ava.

"We're taking it with us in backpacks."

"Really?" said Ava. "You're not joking?"

"Cross my heart it's true," said Sophia, folding her arms over her hoodie. "Ms. Primrose wants us to find the things on the scavenger hunt list as quickly as possible!"

"What's the rush?" said Ava.

"I don't know." Sophia's eyes shone. "But isn't it exciting? Let's go to the lake!"

New friends. New adventures.
Find a new series . . . just for you!